Beet It

Alex Westhaven

Brazen Snake Books
Billings Montana

Beet It

Chapter 1

Tara Pyle knelt in her garden, knees damp under denim overalls, and a wide-brimmed straw hat casting a long shadow over the row where she worked. She pulled a garnet bulb from the soft earth and placed it into the half-full basket at her side, resisting the urge to take a bite of the dirt-encrusted treat, though her mouth watered at the thought.

September was always dry in the high plains of Montana - this year exceptionally so. After a back-breaking summer hauling water back and forth from the not-close-enough spring, she wanted to get the harvest in quickly to avoid watering much more before winter.

Beets were her favorite vegetable. She tucked a stray strand of dishwater blond hair behind her ear and pulled another small red orb from the ground. Flicking a grasshopper off the leaves, she rubbed the root against a long sleeve to knock the dirt off. Raising it to her lips, she sunk her teeth into the earthy treat, closing her eyes and letting the unique flavor dance over her tongue.

Just one wouldn't hurt. She'd planted plenty, and this was the second harvest.

"You look like a vampire."

She wiped the beet juice from the corner of her mouth,

looking up at Colin Yeger, her still-citified boyfriend of three months. He'd moved to Meadowlark just six months ago and asked her out two weeks later. He was mostly easygoing about small town life, but he hadn't quite come to terms with the concept of growing your own food yet. She took in his standard khakis and polo shirt - a blue one today. One of these days, she'd convince him to go shopping with her. The man needed jeans and t-shirts. Maybe a flannel shirt or three. Nothing like a tall, dark-haired man in flannel to get a girl's heart beating faster.

Tara grinned. "Careful. You might be next!"

"I'm not afraid of you." Colin laughed. "I don't trust beets. They're shifty. And that red color is not something you want to see coming out the other end either, if you catch my drift."

"They're vegetables, Col. There's nothing to trust, or not trust. You just eat them. They can't be shifty. They aren't sentient. " She ignored the second comment. He wasn't entirely wrong there.

He shook his head and rocked back on his heels, both hands shoved deep into perfectly pressed pockets. "You're wrong. All vegetables can be evil little buggers. And if you keep eating beets, someday they're going to get revenge. They're out for blood, you know - they suck it out of the soil. That's why they're red."

"That is the stupidest thing I've ever heard. The only thing these beets 'suck' from the soil is fertilizer from my mom's compost." Tara stood up and brushed the dirt off her knees. "Beets are yummy, and very healthy. Pickled, sautéed, boiled... I've never eaten a beet I didn't like. When was the last time you tried one? And what's your stance on other root veggies like carrots? Are they evil too?" She walked over to the carrot section and started pulling up bright orange spears, tucking them in with the beets. Collin followed, his shadow helping to block the sun while she worked.

"I like carrots. They're bright and happy. They don't bleed like beets."

Tara shook her head and sighed. "You are so weird. And I'll have you know I'm sauteing some of these beets for dinner. I expect you to at least try one slice. According to ancient folklore, two people who eat part of the same beetroot will fall in love. Don't you want to fall in love with me?" She laughed as he backed away with his hands up when she thrust the basket toward him. "You don't want to fall in love with me? Come on, Col. Where's your sense of adventure? I'll even bite your neck if you want me to." She winked when she felt like cringing. That last comment might have taken it a bit too far. Thankfully, he laughed, though he was still backing up.

"I've got no problem with you, but I'm not going anywhere with those things. And now you're red-handed. Put them down, quick, and run before the cops come after you!"

Laughing, Tara grasped one beet by the top and pulled it out of the basket, brandishing it like a weapon.

"The beets are on my side, Collin. I think you're the one who'd better...ah...'beet' it. Get it?" He pretended to be scared as she chased him through the back door, dropping the basket on the kitchen counter as she passed through. Collin scrambled over the hardwood floors, through the living room, into the hall and on to the bathroom, slamming the door in her face and securing the lock with a click.

"Now they're making you evil!" he yelled, and if not for the chuckle that followed, Tara might have believed he was actually afraid. "Nothing good will come from eating beets - you'll see!"

Lowering her veg-weapon, Tara leaned against the door, catching her breath.

"I thought you weren't afraid of anything. But here you are, hiding in the bathroom from a lowly beet. Weren't you just saying the other day that you'd take on the entire world to keep me safe if necessary?"

The knob turned, and Tara stepped back just before the door opened enough for Collin to croon at her.

"I would do anything for you... but I won't eat beets."

She burst out laughing. "Okay, okay. Point taken. Are you allergic or something?" She'd never heard of an allergy to beets, but people were allergic to everything these days, it seemed. Not enough playing in the dirt when they were younger, probably.

Collin came out of the bathroom, shaking his head. "Not that I know of. Mom made me try a bite once when I was a kid, and I didn't die or anything. I just don't like them. They taste like dirt."

Tara shrugged. "Okay then. I suppose if you don't want to try again, you don't have to. I'm still going to sauté some for myself, though. Why don't you relax while I make dinner - about an hour and a half. Want a beer?"

He nodded, following her back into the kitchen. When she put the beet back in the basket, his arms slipped around her waist and he nuzzled her neck from behind.

"It's mean to threaten someone with vegetables, you know. I just may retaliate when you're least expecting it." She felt him smile against her skin and she smiled, too.

"You're welcome to try. But you never know when those pesky beets might decide to protect me from you, so careful there, big man."

She pulled away, getting a beer from the fridge and handing it to him. "Now shoo. Leave me in peace with my shifty veggies. I'll let you know when it's safe to come back."

* * *

Alone in the kitchen, Tara started prepping to cook. Colin didn't eat nearly enough vegetables, and she was determined to transform his diet, one hidden veggie at a time. Tonight's meatloaf would contain a couple of fresh grated beets just so she could rub it in later. The earthy flavor would blend right in with the mushrooms, onions and Worcestershire sauce. He wouldn't even know the beets were there until she told him. The look on his face would be priceless.

She grated the beets first, putting them in a glass bowl with ground beef, an egg, some oats and the Worcestershire sauce. Moving quickly, she minced an onion to add, and then chopped a handful of button mushrooms to add as well. Noting a red stain on the side of her thumb, she rinsed it, thinking it was stray beet juice, but when more blood welled up soon after, she realized she'd cut herself.

Frowning, she rinsed it out well with soap and water, and then looked around to make sure she was still alone before she took the leftover end from the beet and held it to the cut.

A few seconds later, her skin was like new - no sign of a cut to be found. Her mother had showed her that trick the day her family had died. The day Tara had found out that the woman she'd known as her aunt Shelley was actually her mom. Presumably Tara had inherited her love of beets and the ability to take advantage of their healing powers from her mother.

5

She tossed the beet end into the compost bucket, then finished shaping the meatloaf on a rack in a shallow pan and put it into the oven with a couple of potatoes to bake.

Wiping down the counters, she cleared the kitchen and set the table, sautéing a pan of green beans and a separate small pan of sliced beets for herself just before the main course was ready. A simple gravy from the pan juices while the meatloaf rested on the counter was her last task before putting everything on the table and slicing thick pieces of the juicy meatloaf to arrange on her favorite white ceramic platter with an array of veggies embossed along the rim.

Colin appeared in the doorway just as she was slicing. "Mmm...it smells too good to wait any longer. Can we eat? I'm starving!"

"Absolutely! Come sit down. I tried a new recipe tonight. You can tell me what you think." She pulled out her normal chair at the end of the table and sat down, waiting for him to sit at her right before she filled her plate.

"There's not enough beets here for both of us," he mocked, handing her the small bowl. She laughed and set the bowl beside her plate, not bothering to transfer the shiny fuchsia medallions out of it.

"Are you sure you don't want to try just one? It could be the turning point in our relationship!"

They both laughed, and she watched a slice of meatloaf disappear bite-by-bite from his plate, and then a second. It was so moist and flavorful - one of her best, for sure. It was definitely going on the to-make-again list.

Colin coughed, then took a drink of water and coughed again, harder. Red blotches were appearing on his face and neck. A cold chill ran down Tara's spine. Something was very wrong here. She couldn't put her finger on it, but her heart raced just like it had when she watched her father, sister, brother and the only mother she'd ever known cough and grab at their throats. *Don't panic*, she reminded herself. *Heimlich. Do it now.*

She got out of her chair and started towards him, but he waved her off, reaching for his throat with his hands.

"Nothing stuck," he wheezed. "Can't breathe. Help." More coughing, and his face was turning to match her beloved beets.

"Oh no. Not again. No, no, no!" Tara grabbed her phone. "Oh god - I'm calling for help. Hang on!" She dialed 9-1-1 and waited impatiently for someone to answer.

No one was picking up. How could 9-1-1 not pick up? Frantic, Tara disconnected and tried to call again, but... nothing. How was that possible? Where were the emergency dispatchers?

Colin fell off his chair, convulsing on the floor. His skin grew redder with hives and in her mind, she saw her brother just before he'd died twenty years before.

"I have to go get help." She hesitated for a microsecond because she didn't want to leave him alone, but then sprinted for the door and yelled over her shoulder, "I'll be right back, I swear! Don't die!"

* * *

Running to the door, Tara flung it open and ran outside. She looked right and left and saw lights at the neighbor's house. Practically flying across the lawn, she ran up the stairs and pounded on the neighbor's door.

"Lynda? Dan? Please - I need help!"

The door opened. She'd never been so relieved to see another person when Dan scowled at her through the storm door. He wasn't her favorite person on account of a drifting pesticide incident several years back, and the feeling was mutual, but right now, he was exactly what she needed.

A warm body, hopefully with a working phone.

"Dan - thank God. I need help! Colin just collapsed on my kitchen floor and I called 9-1-1 but no one answers. Can you call an ambulance? I don't know what else to do!"

"Lynda - call 9-1-1! Have them come next door to Tara's!" He hollered over his shoulder and then stepped outside. "Show me where your friend is."

Tara turned and ran back across the yard, waiting for Dan to catch up before she went through her still-open front door.

"He's just in here," she said, pointing to the dining room table. "There, on the floor." Collin was lying on his side, facing away from them, and she couldn't tell if he was breathing or not. "Oh God," she murmured, hanging back while Dan went to kneel beside Collin. "Oh no. I can't believe this is happening."

Dan shook Collin's shoulder, and when there was no response, pulled him over onto his back. Tara gasped at the bright, beet red color of Colin's skin.

"We need to get out of the house. Now," Dan said. He stood up and reached back down to grasp Collin under the armpits. "Go!" He pulled Colin toward the front door.

"You're not supposed to move someone who needs medical help," she said, following helplessly behind. "I don't hear any sirens. Shouldn't there be sirens by now?"

Dan didn't answer, just dragged Colin out the front door and into the yard. Breathing hard, he motioned for her to move farther away from the doorway where she was still standing.

"Get away from there. Are you feeling okay? Light-headed or dizzy?" He reached out and tugged her forward, examining her skin a little too close for comfort. Tara pulled away and stepped back, shaking her head.

"I'm fine - there's nothing wrong with me. It's Colin. Didn't Linda call 9-1-1?" She looked up and down the street. It shouldn't be taking this long. There was a fire station just three blocks away - why weren't they coming? Or already here?

"I'll go check. Stay here with your friend." Dan ran back to his house and up the front stairs, disappearing behind the storm door.

Tara knelt beside Colin, pressed two fingers against his neck. No pulse.

"Colin? Wake up - talk to me," she whispered. "You can't just die. I don't understand. You said you weren't allergic!"

Collin's chest rose and fell on a single gasp and Tara fell back, one hand going to her own chest. Could it be? Had she just missed the pulse? Moving back onto her knees, she leaned forward, putting her cheek and ear close to his mouth. Why wasn't there any air coming out? Had she just imagined that big breath?

Eeevil beeeeets....

The words drifted soft through the night, a ghost-whisper on the breeze.

When it finally came, the burst of air against her cheek was so cold it burned. She didn't even feel his head move before something moist and sticky ran down the side of her neck. Lifting her head, she watched bright red drops splatter on his skin until the pain finally registered in her brain.

Tara screamed, slamming her hands to her head, the right

one hitting an ear, and the left a warm, sticky wet mess.

Blood ran down her arm in slow motion. The left side of her head pulsed with the beat of her heart, the steady thump drowning out all other sounds in her mind. She swayed on her knees, staring transfixed at a single drop of blood that formed a drop at the end of her elbow, reaching in slow motion for the grass.

Then a dark veil fell across her vision, and she swayed sideways before everything went dark.

Chapter 2

When Tara opened her eyes, the light hurt almost as much as the left side of her head. She groaned, squeezing her eyelids shut to block out the glare and reaching up to press the spot where it hurt. She lay on her back in a narrow bed, and her head wasn't the only thing that hurt.

"Oh my god," she breathed, her fingers finding nothing but a thick mass of bandages covering the spot where her ear should be, and more wrapping around her head to hold the bandages in place. "What the--"

"Oh good - you're awake. Welcome back! We were getting a little worried that we couldn't wake you."

She forcing her eyes open again and turned her head to look at the speaker. A woman stood at the side of the bed in a scrub top covered in tiny unicorns and rainbows, her long brown hair pulled up in a high ponytail and her green eyes overflowing with pity.

"I'm Jackie, your nurse." Her lips curved up in a reassuring smile. "I already paged the doctor, and she can explain everything. In the meantime, do you have any family we can contact? Close friends, maybe? We didn't see any emergency contacts in your file."

Tara shook her head. "Just Colin - the guy I'm seeing. I was with him in the yard... " She couldn't remember anything after she'd leaned down to check his breathing. It all seemed like a bad dream now, fuzzy around the edges. "Where is he? Is he okay?"

"I'm sorry, but I'm afraid your friend didn't make it." A tall, lithe woman with a white coat, a stern bun and expression to match stepped into the room and closed the door behind her. "I'm Dr. Woodrow. Can you tell me the last thing you remember?"

"We were..." The nurse slipped out and Tara stared at her hands. "We were outside, on the lawn. He... he'd collapsed at dinner. My neighbor pulled him outside. I told him we shouldn't move Colin, but he wouldn't listen."

The doctor nodded, busily making notes. "And what about before he collapsed? What were you doing before that?"

"Eating." Tara swiped at her eyes. "I made meatloaf. We sat down to eat, and... I was watching him closely. Waiting for him to take a bite." She gasped and looked up at the doctor, unable to stop the tears now.

"I put beets in the meatloaf. That's the only thing I did differently, and his skin was red - like beet red- when he collapsed. I killed him, didn't I? Oh God! Oh no! This is all my fault!"

Her shoulders shook, and she teared up, but something felt off. She just wasn't sure what.

The doctor gave her a sympathetic look. "You didn't kill your boyfriend."

Tara took a deep breath, swiped at her eyes and reached for a tissue to blow her nose.

"I don't understand. He was fine, and then he couldn't

breathe, and I asked him if he was allergic earlier and he said no...." The tears welled up again, and she didn't care. The doctor took a step closer, her heel clicking sharply on the tile floor.

"The tests aren't back yet, but given what you describe and how he looked when he was brought in, your boyfriend likely died of carbon monoxide poisoning. If your neighbor hadn't gotten you both out of the house so quickly, you wouldn't be here right now."

Tara threw up her hands, frustrated. "That doesn't make any sense. The furnace is brand new, and I just put new carbon monoxide detectors in when I replaced the smoke detector batteries. Maybe a month ago?" She reached for another tissue. "And none of this explains the bandages around my head. Did I fall? I remember running to the neighbors for help and then kneeling in the yard beside Colin. I leaned over to check if he was breathing. After that, everything just sort of fades to black. I didn't even hear the sirens."

Dr. Woodrow patted her shoulder. "When you were trying to help him, Colin was confused. Delirious. Not something we normally see with CO2 poisoning, but certainly not impossible. As far as we can tell, he bit the outer shell of your left ear off just before he died."

Tara heard the words, but they rambled in her brain like a foreign language for all the sense she could make of them.

"He bit my ear off? The whole thing? That's why my head hurts? Were you able to reattach it?"

The doctor shook her head and sighed.

"I'm afraid we weren't able to retrieve the ear in time, and it was... badly damaged by the time medics reached you. Your head will heal, though, and while you'll have some hearing loss on that side due to the outer conch being gone, you will still have some hearing."

Tara frowned. "If it was carbon monoxide, why wasn't I affected? He was so...pink. And it came on so quickly. I didn't feel sick or dizzy or tired or anything while he was gasping for air." She laid her head back against the pillow. "None of this makes any sense."

"You've suffered a lot of trauma in the last twenty-four hours. Why don't you just get some rest, and we'll check the stitches in a couple of hours. If everything looks okay, you can go home tonight."

The doctor turned and walked out, her lab coat swishing against a no-nonsense navy pencil skirt. Tara had always wished she had the figure for one of those skirts.

She looked out the window. The birds were chirping, the sun was shining brightly, her ear was gone and Colin was dead. How was she supposed to be okay with all of that?

And why did it feel like she was more upset about her ear being gone than her boyfriend?

* * *

Tara dozed fitfully in the uncomfortable hospital bed, CNAs checking on her occasionally and her roommate watching old daytime game shows on TV. When the nurse finally came back, she was bored, tired of the constant ringing in her left ear, and getting hungry. At least the pain had subsided. She'd even refused the pain pills they'd offered during the last check.

Nurse Jackie came in with a metal rolling tray holding scissors and new bandages.

"Let's see how your stitches look," she said. "If everything looks okay and clear of infection, we'll put a smaller bandage on it and you'll be free to go home."

Tara nodded, sitting up to allow better access.

The nurse cut the tape and unwrapped the bandages slowly. Tara felt like a mummy, watching everything come off. When it was time to remove the main gauze pad, Jackie stepped back and frowned.

"I'm not really sure how this is even possible," she murmured, frowning. "Let me go get the doctor. I'll be right back." She turned and walked out, coming back in less than two minutes later with the doctor.

Dr. Woodrow took a pen light out of her pocket and then leaned down to examine Tara's eyes, flicking the light back and forth. "How does the side of your head feel?"

Tara shrugged. "Kind of itchy and sore, but otherwise okay. The pain stopped, but my ear won't stop ringing." She almost asked why, but it occurred to her that pickled beets had been served with her lunch. Mystery solved, though not for the doctor.

"Because somehow your wound appears to be almost completely closed around the stitches. I don't think I've ever seen a wound close so fast in the twenty years I've been practicing."

Tara hadn't been to the doctor in years, and this was why. Too many questions she didn't have answers to. And too many doctors who wanted to push it, to figure out what was wrong with her just because she healed faster than the average person.

As long as she had beets in her system, that is.

Dr. Woodrow straightened and put the light back in her pocket. She looked at Nurse Jackie and gestured to Tara's ear.

"Has anyone dressed this wound since last night? Put some kind of ointment on it or something, perhaps?"

The nurse shook her head. "Not that I know of. And I only came in here once today, but I was doing a med pass."

The doctor nodded. "Any visitors that you know of? Can you check the logs for me, please?"

"I'll do that right now. Be right back."

After she left, the doctor picked up a thin pair of scissors from the tray. "We may as well take those stitches out now. Then we'll get you discharged and you can go home, though I'd like to get some extra blood for testing, if you don't mind."

Home. Tara's mind was racing with questions, but going anywhere but here seemed like a good idea. She heard the faint snipping of the scissors and felt the tugs as the doctor pulled the series of knots out.

"Do you know if it's safe?" Tara asked when the doctor finally put the scissors down. "To go home, I mean. You said Colin died of carbon monoxide poisoning. I don't want to go home and die."

"I'm not sure." The doctor wiped something cool over her wound with a cotton round. "There was a detective here asking to speak with you earlier when you were asleep. I can get you his contact information, and you can find out what normally happens after something like this." She cleaned up her tools and pointed to the cupboard. "Your clothes are in there. I'll let you go ahead and get dressed, and the nurse will be in to take another blood sample, and give you that information." She tilted her head, an odd look on her face. "You're the only person I didn't ask about the quick healing, and you don't seem all that surprised. Is there something I should know about here? Some condition you have, maybe?"

Tara shrugged, doing her best to look shell-shocked, though she suspected she wasn't fooling anyone.

"I have no idea, Doc. Your guess is as good as mine." She could tell the doctor wasn't buying it, but her cell phone buzzed, and Dr. Woodrow looked at the screen, and then back at Tara with a neutral expression in place.

"I'll have the nurse set up a recheck appointment in a week. And I'll call you if I find anything on further blood tests. I'm truly sorry about the loss of your friend."

"Thank you." Tara swung her legs over the side of the bed. "And thanks for stitching me up." But the doctor was already on the way out, the door swinging closed behind her.

* * *

After the doctor left, Tara carefully got out of bed and went to the cupboard. She pulled on her clothes and then took her shirt off again, staring at the large bloodstain covering the right shoulder and going down the arm. "I can't wear this," she murmured, reaching back to push the call button. Before she could press it, the nurse came in with plastic caddy of supplies and a slip of paper in her hand. Her smile fell when she saw the shirt Tara was holding.

"Well, you can't wear that out, can you? Do you have anyone who could bring you a clean shirt?"

Tara shook her head. "It's just...uh...no. No, I don't."

The nurse patted her shoulder. "Let's get that extra blood sample the doctor wants, and then I'll check the lost and found. I think there's something that will fit you in there." She held out the piece of paper. "Here's the number for that detective who wanted to speak with you. He should be able to let you know if your house is safe to go back to."

"Thank you." Tara took the paper and sat back on the bed, quiet as the nurse took two vials of blood from her arm. When she left, Tara was so tired she nearly laid back down on the bed. But it was only a couple of minutes before the nurse was back with a plain gray sweatshirt and a paper bag. She held them out with a too-wide smile.

"Here you go! This should fit well enough, and there's a bag for your other one. Just push the call button again when you're ready to check out, and we'll get you all taken care of. Do you have a ride home?" Tara shook her head. "You can call a cab - the number's by the phone."

"I'll get an Uber. Thank you for your help."

After the nurse left, Tara pulled the sweatshirt over her head and picked up her phone. The battery was getting low, so she ordered an Uber and then put it in her pocket, opting for the hospital's land line to call the detective.

"Detective Williams? This is Tara Pyle. The nurse said you called and wanted to speak to me about my boyfriend's death last night. His name was Colin. Colin Yeger."

"Thank you for calling me back, Ms. Pyle. How are you feeling? You had a pretty rough night yourself, from what I hear."

"I'll be okay. I just want to go home." She closed her eyes and rubbed her forehead with her free hand. "The doctors say Colin died of carbon monoxide poisoning. Is that true? Because I felt nothing like he did, and we were literally sitting in the same room. I didn't pass out like he did either - not until later, anyway."

"The autopsy won't be done for a while, and his toxicology screening came back negative for anything out of the ordinary in his bloodstream. We just always assume it's CO_2 when they come in pink like that, but that doesn't mean it's true. I had someone out at your house earlier today and they didn't find any evidence of carbon monoxide in your house. So it seems like it was something else that killed him. Any ideas? Did he have any allergies that you know of - allergies that were bad enough he could have died from them? The lab will test for that too, but anything you could tell us might speed things up."

Tara was quiet for a long moment. "He said he wasn't allergic to beets. I put beets in the meatloaf - that's the only thing that was different about last night. Is it possible that's what killed him? Can you even be allergic to beets?" She sighed and swiped at the tears threatening to fall. What a nightmare. What if she had actually killed him? What if the beets actually were "evil," like he'd said? How could something evil be so helpful and necessary to her?

"Interesting. I don't know if there's a beet allergy or not, but I'll get this information back to the lab, and see if there's any way they can tell whether he was allergic. Once we know that, we'll figure out what's next, though if you didn't know about any allergy ahead of time, then you can't be held responsible. Is this a good number to reach you at?"

"No, this is a hospital phone." Tara looked down at her cell. "My cell is almost dead, but I'll charge it first thing when I get home. I'm leaving soon. I just need to get an Uber."

"You know, I'm only about 5 minutes away. If you don't mind, I can come give you a ride. I'd like to look around your house and yard just a little more, if that's okay with you."

"Of course." Tara rubbed her forehead with her free hand. The last thing she needed was a detective snooping around her house, but better to get it over with now. "Whatever you need. I'll wait down by the main hospital entrance."

* * *

Tara had been waiting about ten minutes when an older model classic sedan in typical police black pulled up in front of the hospital. The man who got out was nothing like she expected. Tall with a blond buzz cut, he was built more like a body-builder than a public servant. She wondered if there were any tattoos under the sharp black jacket stretched too tightly across his shoulders and then blushed at the thought of what else might be under there.

"Tara Pyle?"

She nodded, carefully getting out of the wheelchair they'd insisted she ride out in before she extended a hand to meet his.

"Nice to meet you, Detective Williams. Thanks for the ride. I appreciate it."

"I'm happy to help. Let's get you in the car. We can talk on the way." He turned and opened the passenger door and she got in, feeling strange at being in the front seat of a police vehicle. Not that she'd been in the back since high school.

He closed her door and got in behind the wheel, bringing the engine to life.

"How are you feeling?"

"Weird." Tara reached up to feel the spot where her ear used to be. Other than a small conch-shaped lump under her skin, it was smooth and felt like nothing had happened, though she sensed there was still some healing going on under the skin. A few beets might help speed that along, but for now, it was just as well it wasn't healing any faster, since there was no way to hide it from the detective. Better to play dumb, as usual.

"My ear is gone, but the doc said the wound healed overnight, which isn't supposed to happen. She even took the stitches out before I left today. So not only is my boyfriend dead, I'm apparently a freak of nature now. It's very--"

"Weird," the detective finished. "That's a lot to deal with all at once. So you don't have any pain or scarring on that ear?"

"Just a small lump where it used to be. And I can't hear as well on that side, which the doctor said was normal." She changed the subject. "You're sure the house is safe?"

The detective nodded. "The guys who checked out your place didn't find any trace of CO2 or leaks - they checked the furnace as well, which is standard in cases like these. So it should be safe to stay there. I also checked with the coroner. She's never heard of a beet allergy before, but she's checking with the local hospitals to see if there's a test she can run."

"I asked my doctor - she's going to run those tests as well, so I don't know how all of this works, but your coroner could work with her. She said she'd let me know what they find out." Tara frowned out the window, disturbed that talking about this wasn't upsetting. She should be more upset. Why didn't she feel anything?

"Well, keep me in the loop, and I'll do the same for you." He pulled into her driveway and turned off the engine. "I know this is difficult, but could you walk me through the whole thing now that we're here? Starting with dinner. I want to experience everything through your eyes, so to speak."

"Uh... sure. I can do that." Tara got out of the car and went to the front door, and then stopped, patting her pants pockets for any bulges. "I don't have my keys." She looked down, and then held up one finger. "I think I put a spare here..." Moving into the narrow garden bed beside the house, she bent down to rummage under a thick bush and found the fake rock near the back. Opening a secret compartment in the bottom, she retrieved the spare key and went back to the door.

"I was unconscious when they took me to the hospital." She led him into the house, dropped the bag with her bloody shirt in it on the couch, and led the detective to the kitchen. "It started here. I was making dinner at the counter, and Colin was in the living room watching TV."

"With his back to you."

Tara nodded. "He came into the kitchen when the meatloaf started smelling good, and then we sat at the table - he sits here," she pointed to a chair to her left. "And I sit right here." She grasped the back of the chair facing the living room. "We dished up our plates and ate a few bites. He was telling me how good it was when he started turning red, and then he just collapsed and rolled out of his chair - that way." She pointed to the opposite side of the table.

The detective nodded. He wasn't taking notes or anything, which Tara thought was a little strange, but he was listening intently.

"Is that when you called for help?"

"Yes. I thought he was choking, but he said he wasn't, and pointed to his phone. So I tried to call 9-1-1."

"You tried. Was the phone dead?"

Tara shook her head. "No one answered! I don't understand why no one answered - I didn't even think that was possible."

The detective frowned. "It shouldn't be - ever. Do you remember what time it was?"

She shook her head. "Between seven and seven-thirty or so. I'm sorry I can't be more specific."

He pulled out his phone and typed a note. "That should be close enough. I'll definitely have someone check on that. So what happened next?"

"I ran to the front door and saw the lights on at the neighbor's house, so I ran over there and pounded on the door. Dan came over. He's the one who moved Colin to the yard, and then he went back to make sure his wife called for an ambulance."

The detective nodded. "Can you show me where in the yard your neighbor left you with Colin?"

"Sure -let's go back this way." She led him back through the front door, down the three steps and out onto the lawn between her house and Dan and Lynda's.

"It was right about here," she pointed to a flattened patch of grass with a dark stain just to one side. "Or pretty much exactly here, considering that's... probably my blood."

"Where was the neighbor when that happened?"

"He ran back to his house - we didn't hear sirens yet, so he went to make sure Lynda had called 9-1-1."

"And what's the last thing you remember about being out here alone with Colin?"

"He went still, and I leaned over him to see if he was breathing - you know, like they do on TV. I remember the sensation of raindrops on my head, and red splatters on his face, but that's it." Tara crossed her arms over her chest, trying to control a shiver.

"Next thing I know, I woke up in the hospital and they told

me Colin was dead." She shivered again, her stomach queasy. "Would you mind if we went inside now? I think I need to sit down for a little while."

"Of course." He motioned for her to walk with him toward the house. "I just have one more question, and I'll leave you to rest. I know this is intrusive, but you said they took the stitches out already. May I see the wound?"

Tara turned her head, pulling her hair back with one hand. It was odd not feeling it anchor at the back of her ear, but there was definitely a crescent-shaped ridge where the conch used to be. She didn't mention that the ridge hadn't been there when she left the hospital.

"Wow." The detective gave her a sheepish grin, as if he hadn't meant to say that out loud. "I'm sorry. I just expected it to be a lot less healed. Compared to the pictures I saw from last night, it looks like a remarkable recovery."

Letting her hair fall back down across her face, Tara nodded. "That's what the doctor said, too. I wish I had some sort of explanation for you, but I don't understand it myself." She didn't like lying, but it was her only choice unless she wanted to become a human guinea pig.

Detective Williams pulled a card out of his wallet and handed it to her. "I'll let you rest now, but if you have any questions or need to get in touch with me, feel free to call anytime. I'll let you know when we get the official coroner's report back. I'm sorry for your loss."

"Thank you." Tara took the card and walked with him as far as her front walk. She stood there watching as he drove away, and then went into the house and locked the door.

Chapter 3

Tara woke up some time later on her living room couch in the dark. Groggy, she sat up and ran a hand through her hair, noting how greasy it was. The last thing she remembered was coming inside after Detective Williams had gone and going to the fridge for a snack. There had been some leftover cut veggies, and she'd sat down here on the couch to eat them.

She felt around for the bowl, finding it on the floor with only a few sliced carrots and bits of broccoli in the bottom. There had been beets from her garden and cauliflower as well, she remembered.

Reaching up to scratch an itch on her left ear, she stopped abruptly when her fingers brushed over the bump where the missing conch used to be. She focused, feeling the area again more deliberately. Was she hallucinating, or was the bump larger now?

She picked up the bowl and took it through the dining room table where last night's dinner sat as if they'd just gotten up for a second, and into the kitchen. She put the bowl on the counter and backtracked to the same bathroom Colin had barricaded himself in the day before. Flicking the light switch on, she pulled back the hair on the left side of her head so she could actually see what was going on with her ear.

"It's growing back," Tara murmured, staring in awe at the new conch forming where hers had been severed. "Very cool." She stared for a few minutes more, looking at it from all angles. She'd realized several years ago that beets made her heal faster, but she'd always wondered what would happen if an appendage got severed. If her ear grew back, did that make her invincible?

Tara glanced at the clock on the vanity. It was nearly eleven pm, and she really should go to bed if she was going to make it to work tomorrow.

Had she called work this morning to let them know where she was? Her stomach rumbled as she tried to remember.

Turning out the bathroom light, she went back to the kitchen and checked the fridge. Her stomach gurgled again, but there wasn't really anything readily accessible that looked good. Closing the refrigerator door, she opened the freezer and took out one of her "emergency" frozen meals without paying too much attention to the picture on the cover. Ripping open the box, she stabbed the plastic cover over the compartmentalized plate and placed the unrecognizable substance into the microwave. Three minutes, then two minutes, and she carefully pulled out a somewhat sketchy-looking Salisbury steak with a mound of make-believe mashed potatoes in one side compartment, and a sad-looking pile of corn in the other.

"Some of those beets would be good with this," she murmured, opening the fridge again. Taking one smallish red root out of the crisper, she washed it, put a cutting board on the counter and got a sharp knife. She peeled off the outer skin, cut off the top and root end, sliced the rest into thin slices, and put them in a bowl in the microwave for a couple of minutes before dumping them in beside the steak.

She put the plastic compartmentalized plate on a flat ceramic one for stability and went back to the living room, fork and napkin in hand. Sitting on the couch, she turned on the TV and ate her dinner. The beets were the best part, of course, though mixing the corn into the potatoes salvaged the sides to some extent as well.

When she was done, she took her dishes to the kitchen, left them on the counter, sighed at the mess on the dining room table and went to bed.

* * *

Tara woke to sunshine sneaking through a small crack in her bedroom curtains and her left ear throbbing against the pillow like someone had just punched the side of her head. Groggy and disoriented, she turned to her back and pressed a hand hard to where her left ear should have been, willing the pain to stop. Her focus shifted quickly though when her finger traced the defined outer edge of an ear conch where the small bump had been last night, though it was still too small to be considered the outer part of an ear.

With a groan and a wince, she forced herself to get up and stumble to the bathroom. Blinking as she flipped the light on, she stared at the mirror above the sink until her brain could process what she was seeing.

There, where the small ridge had developed behind her ear yesterday, was the mirror image of the ear on the other side of her head. It was about a third the size of her normal ear, but it definitely matched, and the edges had flatted out and curled in on top, just as one would expect.

She ran her fingers over it, gently feeling each part of the newly formed ear. The skin was super-soft, and her light touch tickled the sensitive new tissue. Underneath, it ached, which made sense considering everything that was apparently going on.

"Unbelievable," she murmured, turning her head one way, and then the other, comparing her good ear with the regenerating one. "I can't believe this is happening."

She just barely heard the phone ringing from the bedroom and looked at the clock.

"Great. Late again."

She ran to the bedroom and answered the call on the third ring. As she thought, it was her boss, and after an odd conversation about what had happened with Colin and her ear, she hung up fifteen minutes later with the rest of the week off and her boss's 'sincere condolences'.

"What is wrong with me?" She slumped down on the bed and let the phone fall to the mattress. Why had she thought going to work was a good idea? Why hadn't she called in earlier? Why didn't she feel... much of anything when she told people about Colin?

Her boyfriend had died barely two days ago, and she'd been planning on getting ready for work as usual this morning. Tara wasn't sure what she'd been thinking, but it didn't seem right that she wasn't crying over losing someone she loved. She'd loved Colin.

Hadn't she?

"It has to be shock," she murmured, forcing herself to get up and go to the closet. "I'm sure it just hasn't set in yet. It will hit me anytime now." She pulled on a clean pair of underwear and jeans, a sweatshirt without stains that didn't smell, and a clean pair of socks. Padding out to the kitchen, she went through the motions of setting up the coffee pot and while that was brewing, she emptied the dishwasher and cleaned up the mess on the table from that last dinner.

Evil beeeeetssss....

She dropped a plate as Colin's last words seemed to drift on the air. Ceramic chips flew every which way as the plate broke into three pieces, one of them bouncing off her foot. She stood and stared down at the gash left behind by the sharp edge. Blood oozed out and trailed down to the floor. It took a few seconds for the actual pain to register, and she shook when it hit, her stomach queasy. Sliding to the floor, she reached out and grabbed the towel hanging off the stove handle. She wrapped it around her foot and squeezed hard, wanting... needing to stop the blood.

A red spot grew over the cut, and her mind kept flashing to the red dripping on Colin's face. The side of her head ached, and her neck felt wet and warm, just like it had the night before. Keeping one hand on the towel, she lifted a hand to her neck, expecting to feel that familiar wet and sticky texture. But her neck was dry. There was no blood when she pulled her fingers away, and she closed her eyes, leaning her head back against the cupboard.

Her foot was throbbing, her ear was throbbing, and Tara could hear her own heartbeat thump with each pulse of blood through her skin. The sound grew louder and louder and she slumped lower against the cabinets, her head spinning as the room went dark.

When she came to, she was lying on her side on the kitchen floor. Disoriented, she pushed up to a sitting position, feeling the towel slide from her foot as she did. Everything that had happened earlier came back in a rush, and she sat up, wondering how long she'd been laying there.

Then she unwrapped the bloody towel from her foot and blinked hard. There was no gash, no blood. The top of her foot looked perfect. Or normal, anyway.

Taking a couple of deep breaths, she got to her feet and retrieved a broom and dustpan, cleaning up the broken plate bits still scattered over the floor. Once that was done, she finished loading the dishwasher. Then Tara poured herself a cup of coffee and went to the back porch to drink it.

From the porch swing, she could see the whole half-acre that had come with the house. That and the already established gardens had been why she'd bought it in the first place. Her gaze drifted over the wooded area in back and across to the veggie gardens neglected for two days now. She'd need to water, and there were onions, carrots and more beets to harvest as well.

Her mouth watered at the mere thought of the juicy red beets. *Need beets....*

She tried to banish the voice as quickly as it flitted through her mind. But she couldn't, anymore than she could cut off her own arm.

* * *

Tara finished her coffee and went back inside for a refill. Her phone was ringing on the counter, and after checking the screen, she answered.

"Good morning Detective. I didn't expect to hear from you again so soon."

"Good morning. I got the coroner's tox report back and wanted to get you the results right away. She fast-tracked it for us, given the potential danger of a toxin in your house. The good news is, it definitely wasn't carbon monoxide that killed Mr. Yeger, and he definitely wasn't allergic to beets. There was an odd compound in his blood that we can't identify, though, which is concerning. Our forensics lab has been working with the hospital lab on this, and they'd like to test your blood for the same substance, if you don't mind. They can use one of the extra vials your doctor collected if you give your permission."

"Of course." She was curious, but also wary. This is how it started. She needed to talk to her mom and make sure she had a good answer ready, in case they requested further testing. "Is there anything else I can do for you, detective? I'm kind of tired. I need to go lay down soon."

"Just one more thing." He paused. "Do you know how to get in touch with Colin's parents or family? We can't seem to find any contact information for them."

Tara shook her head, even though he couldn't see her. "He said his parents had been dead for a long time when we met. And no brothers or sisters, either. It was just him, or that's what he told me."

The detective didn't respond right away, and she got the feeling he didn't believe her, but she was telling the truth. Colin had told her on their second date that he didn't have any family. She could only share what she knew.

"Thank you for your help," he finally said. "Get some rest, and I'll be in touch as soon as I know more."

Disconnecting the call, Tara went back to the back porch and sat in an over sized wicker chair to finish her coffee. She'd met

Colin in a nightclub, and after swearing never to pick a guy up at a bar, she'd brought him home the first night. There had been something magnetic about him, something that drew her in, even though he really wasn't her type.

Now she was wondering what she'd ever seen in him. It didn't make any sense, but it was like he'd turned into a stranger overnight. Unsettling, considering how just twenty-four hours ago she was hoping their 'crush' would turn in to a long-lasting love just by eating part of the same root vegetable. Maybe the folklore had worked in reverse - eating from the same beet had severed the relationship rather than made them fall in love. But it was all just an old story... wasn't it?

With a heavy sigh, she went to the kitchen, put the cup on the counter, and decided to take a shower. Maybe the hot water would provide the perspective she needed, and after, she'd call her mom.

* * *

Tara had never been close to Shelley, but she needed to talk to someone, and her mom was the only person on the planet who would understand. Shelley was the only family Tara had left, and also the only other person she knew affected by beets the same way.

There were rumors she'd been an addict of some sort and spent time in a mental institution when Tara was very young, which is why Tara had lived with her father and his wife. Shelley didn't talk about it, and Tara knew not to ask. Even after Shelley had gotten out, Tara had seen little of her until that Thanksgiving, when Shelley had come for dinner, and everyone else had died.

She'd moved back in with Shelley then, but only until she'd finished school. They'd lived largely separate lives even then, and Tara had never really felt that mother-daughter bond with her.

Still, she was always willing to help when Tara needed her, and today, Tara definitely needed some guidance. She dialed the number, and Shelley picked up on the first ring.

"Hi Tara - this is a nice surprise. How are you?"

Tara didn't mince words, knowing her mom could handle and preferred directness.

"I think I'm going crazy. Colin died the other day, and it was weird. He was eating dinner with me, and then just fell off his chair, turned bright red, and died. But he bit my ear off right before, and you're not going to believe it, but my ear is growing back! There wasn't even a stump left, and now it's almost back to normal. I know beets are healing for us, but I didn't know we could regrow whole parts of our bodies! And why don't I feel sad or sorry that Colin's gone? I should feel something, right?"

"You're not crazy, my dear. I think it's time we had a talk. Can you come over for dinner tonight? Around seven?"

"I can do that. Should I bring anything?"

"Some fresh beets from the garden, if you have them."

"I can pull some. I'll see you soon. Thanks Shelley."

Chapter 4

Shelley lived a few miles out of town, and there was an extra car at the cottage when Tara pulled into the long, circular gravel drive that night. She didn't recognize it, and it annoyed her a little that her mom had invited someone else. She got the bag of beets she'd pulled from the back seat and breathed in the scent of honeysuckle as she walked up to the teal-colored door. It opened before she could knock.

"Come in, come in." Shelley smiled and patted her shoulder as Tara stepped into the small, warm living room. "I've asked someone to join us. You remember Randall Jones?"

Tara frowned. "My old boyfriend from college? How do you even know him, and what's he doing here?" She handed the beets to her mom.

Shelley grinned. "You'd be surprised at the things I pay attention to, my dear. Just trust me. This will all work out for the best in the end. Now you stop in the dining room and say 'hi' to Randall, and then come help me in the kitchen. Don't be long. I think you'll find tonight very...informative."

Giving her mom a sidelong glance as the woman disappeared down the hall, Tara walked between two overstuffed couches to the other side of the room and peeked around the open french doors into the dining room. That was her old boyfriend sitting by himself at the long, mahogany table all right, and as far as she could see, he hadn't changed a bit. In fact, she was pretty sure he'd had that exact army green band t-shirt on the day he broke up with her over a decade ago, though it had fit better then. How the hell had her aunt found him, and why invite him to dinner? Maybe he was rich, though she doubted it, given how he was eyeing the silver candlesticks at either end of the table.

She leaned back and closed her eyes for a second, gathering strength. The last thing she needed was a blast from her past, much less one who she'd hoped to never see again.

"Tara? Is that you? Whoa - you look great! All 'adult' and stuff. Looks good on you, babe."

She opened her eyes to find Randy grinning at her from the doorway, close enough she could smell his breath and see the comb-over he had going on. Not something anyone should be subjected to. The guy she'd practically worshiped in college now just looked like a sad, middle-aged version of the kid. It wasn't a good look.

"Randy. What are you doing here? You look exactly the same as you did in college. How did that arts degree work out for you? Weren't you going to be a comic book illustrator?"

"I'm still drawing, got some freelance marketing art gigs here and there. Can't seem to get anyone interested in hiring me, but I'm doin' okay, runnin' tabletop games at the comic shop on the weekends. Buddy offered me a couch for the summer, so I'm staying with him until I get a job good enough to pay rent. Or a new girlfriend to bunk with." He winked.

As if.

She gave him a dubious smile. "I...uh...need to go help Shelley in the kitchen. If you want to sit down, I'm sure we won't be long."

"Cool, cool." He sauntered back to the table, and Tara walked around the other side and through the swinging door in the opposite wall to get some answers.

* * *

"Seriously," she said when she walked into the kitchen. "What is he doing here? He was hitting on me - already!"

Shelley laughed at Tara's exaggerated shudder. "Calm down, dear. You won't have to worry about him for long." Her aunt pointed to a wooden cutting board on the kitchen counter. "Go ahead and peel those beets you brought and then grate them down. We're doing an experiment with a new dish tonight - cabbage rolls with a sort of gravy instead of tomato sauce. I think the flavor will compliment the beef and cabbage nicely."

"Sounds good." Tara took the beets out of the bag and washed them. "So the beets are going into the stuffing?"

Shelley nodded. "I think they'll add a nice flavor, don't you? You can add them to that pan of ground beef on the stove when you're done. Then the stuffing will be ready."

It didn't take long for Tara to add the beets, and as she stirred the mixture, it felt like a knot was forming in her chest.

"I don't know if this is such a good idea," she said, staring at the same basic ingredients she'd made for Colin. Her mom's stuffed cabbage was basically just meatloaf rolled in cabbage leaves, after all. She put the wooden spoon down and backed away. "They said it wasn't the beets, but what if it was? We could all die."

Shelley gently pushed her out of the way. "That's not going to happen, dear. You and I will be just fine, I promise. Now get one of the smaller spoons from the drawer by the sink and let's get these cabbage leaves stuffed. We don't want to leave our guest waiting for too long now, do we?"

"What is he doing here, anyway? I haven't seen him in years, and now he's sitting in your dining room? How do you know him?"

Shelley finished stuffing the pre-boiled cabbage leaves and ladled a rich-looking gravy over the top, putting the whole pan in the oven and turning the heat to four hundred twenty-five degrees.

"I actually ran into him at the store the other day, if you can believe that. We got to chatting, and when I mentioned I had a daughter that went to the same college, one thing led to another. Now we need to let these warm through for just a few more minutes. I have a veggie tray in the fridge - let's take that out to our guest with some drinks."

* * *

Twenty minutes later, Tara was relieved when the buzzer on the stove went off. Randy was such a bore that she couldn't imagine what she'd ever seen in him, and she would have done just about anything to get him out of the house and out of her life again. How anyone managed to stall that badly in life and still... exist was beyond her comprehension.

"I'll get dinner Tara, if you want to clear off the appetizer dishes."

Shelley went to the kitchen and Tara dutifully gathered the remains of the veggie tray along with the small plates they'd been using. She put them in the kitchen near the sink and grabbed a large serving spoon from a large porcelain pitcher that held several cooking and serving implements.

"I'm not sure how much more of this I can take," she murmured.

The woman just smiled. "I think it will all be over soon."

They went back to the table and Shelley plated up a couple of steaming cabbage rolls for each of them, ladling extra sauce over the top.

"Now eat up, and don't be shy," she said, picking up her fork and knife. "This is a new recipe, and we both want to know what you think."

"It smells divine." Tara took a long sniff and closed her eyes. "Beefy and...rich." She took a bite and smiled. "I think you've outdone yourself this time, Shelley."

Randy took a bite too and stopped mid-chew to give a little moan. "Wow. This is amazing!" He ate quickly, finishing his whole plate in the time it took Tara and Shelley to each finish one roll. "Can I have another?" He held his plate out.

Shelley smiled and took his plate. "Of course! I'm glad you like it." She dished up one more cabbage roll for him and handed the plate back. "Enjoy!"

Randy attacked the food like he hadn't eaten in three days. Tara looked at Shelley and raised an eyebrow. Shelley just winked.

And then it happened.

Tara felt her stomach drop as Randy's silverware dropped to the plate, clattering loudly before it bounced off the table and to the floor. He followed shortly, his shoulders tensing and his face freezing into a horrible grimace as he fell sideways to the floor and started to convulse.

"Oh no! Not again!" Tara put her utensils down, moving to go to him.

Shelley put a hand on Tara's wrist and shook her head. "Leave him. It'll be over soon. There's nothing you can do now, anyway - believe me. I know. Finish your dinner. You'll need your strength to help me clean up."

Tara stared at her mother, eyes wide and heart racing. "You knew this would happen? How? What did you do?" Randy was still twitching on the floor, his skin turning the same fuchsia color that Colin's had been.

"I did a little experiment," Shelley said. "You needed to know, and now you do. It is the beets, Tara. Or rather, a combination of the beets and the person who grows them. If we'd used beets from my garden, the same thing would have happened. But beets from the neighbor's garden would have been safe for our friend here."

Tara looked from her mom, who had just taken another bite of cabbage roll, to Randy, who had finally stopped convulsing on the floor. His body wasn't slack just yet, and he opened his eyes, pinning her with them. Silently begging for help.

She pushed back from the table, but Shelley stood and grabbed her shoulders before she could move.

"You don't want to get near him right now. After the seizure and just before they die, they get a little... frisky. They know what killed them - I don't know how, and they're looking for revenge. You have a little experience with that."

Tara slumped back into her chair. "Like biting an ear off, you mean?"

Shelley nodded, her expression sympathetic. "How is your ear? Is it healing... well? Any abnormalities?"

"Just that it grew back." Tara moved her hair back, revealing the nearly full-size ear. "The doctor didn't recognize it the next morning, and had to cut the stitches out right away. Has that happened to you, too? How do you know all this? Is it something genetic?"

"I'm not entirely sure, honestly." Shelley put her silverware on her now-empty plate and stood, stacking up Randy's dishes. "I know I heal quickly and without medical attention in most cases, and that beets that I - and now you - grow and serve are toxic to other people, while beets from other gardens are benign. I don't do anything special to grow them, nothing particular with watering or soil, so I have no idea what's causing it, and I had no idea it was genetic until you called the other day with your terrible news. It was then I knew we needed to do an experiment. And unfortunately, I was right."

Tara looked at Randy again. His body had gone slack, his eyes still open, but lifeless.

"I think he's dead."

She found herself in an awkward spot of caring and not caring. The beets she'd grown had killed this man, but she hadn't known that would happen. Still, she was complicit in taking a life now. She hadn't tried to save him, hadn't called the police or an ambulance. She'd just stood by and chatted with her mother while the life drained out of him.

"Don't overthink it," Shelley warned, stepping past Tara to reach down and close Randy's eyes. "You'll drive yourself insane. I wrestled with this... whatever you want to call it... for many years, several of them spent in a psych ward when you were very young. You don't want to do that, believe me."

"How do I stop it?" Tara followed Shelley into the kitchen with the rest of the dishes. "Do I just stop growing and serving beets?

I can do that, I guess. I don't want to hurt anyone else. I definitely don't want to kill anyone else."

Shelley put her stack of dishes in the sink and pointed to the counter for Tara to set down the rest. "Have you noticed you crave beets? Start thinking about them when you haven't had any in several hours? Eat them raw out of the fridge late at night because it's the only thing that sounds good? Preserve enough for the winter because beets from the store just don't take that edge off like yours do?"

Tara nodded. "All the time. I eat at least some every single day. I feel weak and disoriented when I don't. Are you saying we're addicted to them?"

"You could put it that way, I guess. We need them to stay functional. Those years in the psych ward were some of the worst in my life. As soon as I got out and ate some beets that had survived in my garden, my whole attitude and outlook changed. It was like clouds that had been holding my head hostage dissipated, and I could finally 'think' again."

"Why beets?" Tara followed Shelley back out to the dining room and helped her spread a tarp out beside the body. "When did you first notice it? I didn't even know until Colin. I mean, I noticed I could heal quickly, and that I liked beets a lot, but I had no idea I actually needed them. Or that serving them to someone else would be toxic. How have I made it this long without killing anyone?"

"Help me roll him into it. I don't know why it's just beets - I'm not a scientist. One-two-three." They rolled the body onto the tarp and folded the sides over. "I just know that before the day your family died, I didn't know the beets I grew could kill other people, and after that, I literally drove myself crazy trying to figure out what had happened. I was going through some of your grandma's old things when I finally figured out the secret, and that both she and her mother had been dependent on them too. I tried to commit suicide twice after that, but as you've experienced, it's hard for us to die."

"So you're the reason my whole family died." Tara wasn't sure how to feel. This woman had killed her whole family, and here she was, killing again just to experiment, and not acting like it was only the second time. What wasn't Shelley telling her? "Did grandma say why the beets we grow are toxic to other people?"

"She only wrote that the beets we grow are a special strain of beets developed long ago by our ancestors. And they require special fertilizer to be at their best. Grab that end - we'll drag him out the back door." Shelley waited for Tara to pick up her end of the tarp, and they started dragging the body through the house. "I will regret bringing the beets that Thanksgiving for as long as I live. I didn't want to see anyone in your family die, and I worked very hard to stay out of jail so you wouldn't be alone, especially since I knew you'd need me if this day ever came."

Tara struggled to lift her end up and over as Shelley pulled and tugged the canvas out onto the back porch. When it was finally out, both women dropped the ends for a moment to stand and stretch.

"Now I know why they call it dead weight," Tara said. "What are we going to do with him?"

"See the shed back there?" Shelley gestured toward the back of the property, and Tara could see a dark green building that blended in well with the trees and brush. "We'll take him down there. It's time for you to learn the rest of the family secret." She wiped an arm across her brow and looked down at the canvas body-roll. "I have a flat cart that will work better for this. I'll go get it."

Tara watched her mom go down the back stairs and toward the fence to the left side of the yard. There was a huge pile of firewood there, and she disappeared behind it for a few long seconds, and then emerged with a flatbed cart in tow. She pulled it back to the base of the stairs and anchored it sideways to the bottom one before she came back up on the porch.

"Ready?"

Tara took a deep breath in and let it out slow, trying to process everything she was learning, and not sure she really wanted to know the rest even though she knew she needed to.

"Ready as I'll ever be."

* * *

Tara helped Shelley drag the body down the stairs and onto the flat cart, vowing with each step never to move a body again. But her mom seemed to know exactly what she was doing, which was... unsettling.

"How many times have you done this?" Tara wasn't sure she wanted to know the answer, but she had to ask.

"I do it as needed." Shelley pushed and Tara pulled the cart as well as she could manage, across the backyard and behind the dense thicket to the doors of the nearly-hidden shed. Shelley took out a key ring and unlocked the three padlocks that secured the door.

"This is going to be unpleasant," Shelley warned. "You need to promise me you won't scream, and that if you feel like throwing up, you'll run outside to do it so you don't contaminate anything. Understood?"

Tara nodded, the knot in her stomach pulling tighter. "Maybe I shouldn't see this," she said. "I'm not really sure I want to know what's going on here."

Shelley gave her a sad smile. "I'm afraid you have to know, Tara. The beets won't grow without fertilizer, and this is how we have to make it. When I'm gone, it will be up to you to make your own so you can grow enough beets to supply your own needs. Otherwise you will go insane. It's our family curse."

Tara nodded and stood back while Shelley pulled the door open. It was dark inside, so she couldn't see anything right away, but a distinct coppery smell mixed with the scent of fresh-turned earth wafted out and hung in the air.

"You should be able to push the cart from here. Follow me." Her mom led her inside and as soon as they passed the threshold, a motion-activated light came on. Tara gasped, her stomach churning as her mind processed what she was seeing.

Troughs like the kind she'd seen in westerns for watering horses lined the center path on either side, four in total. Slanting into them were big sheets of wood covered in thick white plastic, with ropes attached to each board. The first one on the right had several small animals tied by their back feet to the ropes, head-down as they lay lifeless on the board. The second and third boards each had a deer, also tied by their back legs, and the fourth was empty.

All the animals had their throats cut, and the stains on the plastic told Tara that they'd bled out into the troughs below.

At the back of the shed, there were two large bins, and a pipe from the bottom of each trough fed into them.

"It's the blood," Shelley said. Tara looked at her in disbelief, unable to speak. "The blood is the essential ingredient in the compost. The rest of the bodies are broken down too, eventually, so nothing goes to waste. But the blood is the most important part. Without that, you and I go literally insane."

Tara shook her head, backing away. "No. No, I can't do this. I won't. You're already insane."

Shelley held up one finger. "Listen. They'll tell you. This is what we have to do."

The breeze blew, and Tara heard the clearly whispered command.

Feeeed beeeets....

Chapter 5

She turned and ran outside, bending over some bushes a few feet from the door to throw up. When she was done, her mother was there, holding out a paper towel.

"I know it's hard. And I didn't want to believe it either. But I don't want you to go through what I did, locked up and miserable. It will get easier, I promise."

Tara jumped as her cell rang in her pocket. She checked the number.

"It's Detective Williams. I have to take this."

Shelley shook her head. "Don't answer it, hon. You need to stay as far away from them as possible. They can't find out about this."

Tara stepped away and answered the call, earning a stern glare from her mother.

"Detective Williams. More news?"

"Yes, actually. I was just calling to let you know we got the test results back, and the same substance we found in Colin's blood was in your sample, too. They're doing some testing, but they could use a larger sample. I guess it's really giving them a hard time trying to identify what it is, exactly, and why it's affecting you differently. Would you mind stopping by the hospital later and giving us one more sample so the lab guys can sort this out?"

Tara nodded slowly. "Sure, I can do that. I'm just finishing some things up, but I'll stop by after."

"There's one more thing." The detective paused. "The substance we found in your blood and Colins was a match to what they found in the samples when your family died as well. I understand your mother refused to give a sample. Would you mind asking if she'd give one now? It would really be good to get a complete picture of what's going on here."

Tara glanced at her mom, who was pointedly looking away, giving her space.

"I don't think she'll agree to that, Detective. Do they have any idea at all what the substance might be?"

"Unfortunately, no. But they want to figure it out, and they need your help to do that."

"Understood. I'll be there soon."

Tara disconnected and went back to her mom. "He wants me to give them another sample." She paused, looking past her mom into the shed. "I want to give it to them. I want them to figure out what this is so we can find another way. This," she gestured to the bodies, "is no way to live."

Shelley put her hands on her hips and looked down at the ground for a long moment. She sighed and shook her head, then moved to stand right in front of Tara.

"This thing that we have with the beets - it's a secret our family has passed down for generations. If you read your grandma's journals, you'll see that women have tried to find another way, and it never ends well. It's a curse, and one I can't allow you to expose, because if they know about you, they'll come after me too. Which is why I have to do this."

Quicker than Tara could react, Shelley pulled out a knife and drew it across Tara's neck. It didn't even hurt; it was so quick and deep. But she could feel her blood spilling out as she reached for her neck and fell to her knees, grasping her throat as the warm life both spilled out and choked her at the same time.

"I hope if there's a next life, you'll forgive me."

The last thing Tara saw was her mother bending down to wipe the blood off her knife in the grass.

* * *

Feeeeed beeeets...

"No. You can't have this one." Shelley put the switchblade back in her pocket. Flicking a stray tear away from her cheek, she went into the shed and made quick work of hanging the man's body on the fourth board, cutting his throat to let the blood run into the trough. Then she locked the doors, loaded Tara's body on the cart with a shovel, and spent the next hour burying her daughter in the meadow just beyond the thicket.

Come feeeeed...

The voices whispered in her head as she passed the vegetable garden on her way back to the house, but she had to make sure the house was clean first, in case the detective came looking for Tara.

Feeeeed for streeength....

Shelley stopped at the last row of beets and sighed. Stooping down, she pulled one from the earth and rubbed the dirt off the red bulb as she continued walking toward the house. She was feeling a little weak from her efforts. Fortification was probably a good idea.

The beets were always right.
She wished they weren't.

* * *

A week later, the moon was full and the night eerily still as Shelley lay in bed. The detective had finally come looking for Tara, and Shelley had graciously made him some of Tara's special-recipe meatloaf.

She woke from a sound sleep to find Tara standing beside her bed, an ax raised over her head.

"You didn't drain all the blood, Mom. I won't make the same mistake."

About the Author

Alex Westhaven is the pseudonym of Jamie DeBree, an author from Billings, Montana. She resides there with her husband and two over-sized lap dogs. Halloween is her favorite holiday, and she has more than her fair share of skeletons (and other body parts) in the closet. For information on upcoming books, visit AlexWesthaven.com or BrazenSnakeBooks.com.

Other books by the author

Death by Veggies

Jack
Sprouted
Lettuce Prey

* * *

Novels

Angel Eyes
When She Cries

* * *

Short/Flash Fiction

Canvas
No Hazard Pay
* * *